MW01178394

AMERICAN MX

From backwater to world leaders

John Perritano

x1000r/min

CRABTREE PUBLISHING COMPANY
www.crabtreebooks.com

Crabtree Publishing Company

www.crabtreebooks.com

Coordinating editor: Chester Fisher
Series and project editor: Shoreline Publishing Group LLC
Author: John Perritano
Series Consultant: Bryan Stealey
Project Manager: Kavita Lad
Art direction: Rahul Dhiman
Design: Ranjan Singh
Cover Design: Ranjan Singh
Photo research: Akansha Srivastava
Editor: Adrianna Morganelli

Acknowledgments

The publishers would like to thanks the following for permission to reproduce photographs:

p4: Simon Cudby; p5: Simon Cudby (all); p6: Topical Press Agency\ Getty Images; p7: Hulton-Deutsch Collection/CORBIS (left); p7: Terry Good Collections (right); p8: Paul Webb Photography (top); p8: Terry Good Collections (bottom); p9: Terry Good Collections (all); p10: Racer X Archives; p11: Racer X Archives; p12: Randy Petree; p13: Randy Petree (all); p14: Simon Cudby (all); p15: Simon Cudby; p16: Simon Cudby; p17: Simon Cudby (all); p18: Simon Cudby; p19: Simon Cudby (all); p20: Simon Cudby (all); p21: Simon Cudby; p22: Simon Cudby (all); p23: Paul Buckley; p24: Simon Cudby; p25: Simon Cudby; p26: Racer X archive; p27: Simon Cudby (top); p27: Racer X Archive (bottom); p28: Simon Cudby; p29: p30: Randy Petree; p31: Racer X Archive

Cover image and title page image provided by Steve Bruhn

Library and Archives Canada Cataloguing in Publication

Perritano, John
      American MX / John Perritano.

(MXplosion!)
Includes index.
ISBN 978-0-7787-3986-9 (bound).--ISBN 978-0-7787-3999-9 (pbk.)

      1. Motocross--United States--Juvenile literature. 2. Motocross--Juvenile literature. I. Title. II. Series.

GV1060.12.P47 2008   j796.7'56   C2008-901221-6

Library of Congress Cataloging-in-Publication Data

Perritano, John.
      American MX / John Perritano.
         p. cm. -- (MXplosion!)
      Includes index.
      ISBN-13: 978-0-7787-3999-9 (pbk. : alk. paper)
      ISBN-10: 0-7787-3999-6 (pbk. : alk. paper)
      ISBN-13: 978-0-7787-3986-9 (reinforced library binding : alk. paper)
      ISBN-10: 0-7787-3986-4 (reinforced library binding : alk. paper)
      1. Motocross--United States--Juvenile literature. 2. Motorcycles, Racing--United States--Juvenile literature. I. Title. II. Series.

GV1060.12.P47 2008
796.7'56--dc22
                                                                              2008006380

Crabtree Publishing Company

Published in Canada
Crabtree Publishing
616 Welland Ave.
St. Catharines, ON
L2M 5V6

Published in the United States
Crabtree Publishing
PMB16A
350 Fifth Ave., Suite 3308
New York, NY 10118

Published in the United Kingdom
Crabtree Publishing
White Cross Mills
High Town, Lancaster
LA1 4XS

Published in Australia
Crabtree Publishing
386 Mt. Alexander Rd.
Ascot Vale (Melbourne)
VIC 3032

Contents

In the Fast Lane

Motocross racing is a wild and bumpy ride over rough dirt tracks. The sport's rise to popularity in America has been almost as bumpy!

On the Track

With 20 riders lined up side by side, the first turn is always the trickiest. The heart pounds. Muscles tighten. This is where Chad Reed longs to be. As the winter sun sets on Anaheim's Angel Stadium, Reed jockeys for position around that first turn. Reed was a near unknown only a few years ago in the world of **supercross**, the in-stadium version of the outdoor races. But on this January night, as the Amp'd Mobile AMA supercross Series gets under way, the first curve on the track belongs to the dark-haired Australian. As Reed's Yamaha motorcycle skids around the corner, James Stewart and Ricky Carmichael—two of the top racers in the United States—are just seconds behind, their front tires eyeing the back of Reed's Yamaha. A cascade of booming fireworks lights the dark southern California sky as Stewart and Carmichael give it the gas.

James Stewart, a top American motocross rider, breaks out of the pack at a 2007 supercross event.

Supercross Action

If a racer isn't careful, the lead in the fast-paced, gear-grinding world of motocross is shaky at best—like a brilliant meteor that fizzles quickly. That's what happens on the lap two. As they make their second pass around the track, Reed drops into second place and Stewart takes the lead. Stewart holds that lofty position around lap three as Reed and Carmichael stay ever so close to Stewart. Then Carmichael crashes, giving the high-flying Stewart the win after 20 bone-jarring, nail-biting laps. Forty-five thousand screaming fans—including singer Michelle Branch and rapper Li'l Jon—yell as Reed, Stewart, Carmichael, and the other racers fly through the air at incredible heights and speeds. It's just another high-flying', heart-stopping' day on the American motocross circuit.

Superstar rider Ricky Carmichael excelled in both the indoor and outdoor forms of this high-speed, dirt-churning motor sport.

Australian Chad Reed shows off the midair form that is part of most motocross racing. Drivers "get air" going off jumps located along the race course.

5

The British Influence

Americans love their motocross, but they can thank their speed-loving friends "across the pond" in Great Britain for cranking up the dirt-churning action, which roared into life in the 1920s.

Scramble Kicks Things Off

For race fans, motocross is bigger than baseball and more fabulous than football. American fans love the speed, the power, the noise, and the action of these racing spectacles. And any motocross race has all the excitement of the World Series and Super Bowl fused into one. While American racers such as Stewart, Carmichael, and Jeremy McGrath have dominated the sport for years, motocross is chiefly a British invention. The sport began in 1924 just outside London in a race known as the Southern Scott Scramble. It featured 80 riders racing 50 miles (80 km) on

Here's a rare action photo from a motocross race held in England in 1924. Riders prowled over the dirt country roads on machines less powerful than today's bikes.

a rugged 2.5-mile (4-km) course. The rules were simple. The first rider to cover the course in the least amount of time won the race. Arthur Sparks was victorious that day, finishing the course in more than two hours. His average speed: 24 miles (38 km) per hour.

Scrambles Spread Out

From that day on, the so-called motorcycle scramble became popular throughout the rest of Great Britain, Belgium, and France. At the same time that the scrambles were spreading across Europe, motorcycle racing was beginning to take root in the United States. While British scrambling featured riders bounding down rough, rocky terrain, the Americans raced on dirt tracks. During the same year that Arthur Sparks won the Southern Scott Scramble, a group of motorcycle enthusiasts formed the American Motorcyclist Association, whose job was to **promote** motorcycle riding in the United States.

No Rules

Early motocross racing did not have many rules. The bikes back then lacked brakes, and riders flew across the course at top speed! The era of American motorcycle racing began in earnest during the fall of 1966. That's when Torsten Hallman came to the United States. Hallman was a world-class racer from Sweden, and had become the king of motocross in Europe. Hallman and his Husqvarna motorcycle thrilled American race fans. A decade later, American racers began winning at the world level. Today, the Americans rule motocross, which looks nothing like the original scrambles of Arthur Sparks' days.

Early scrambles like this one took riders through creeks and up and down rough unpaved roads.

Great Britain was a dominant force in early motocross, and Jeff Smith was one of the country's fastest racers.

Moto Fact

The name motocross comes from the words 'motorcycle' and 'cross-country.'

Edison Dye's Flying Circus

Motocross was catching on in Britain and Europe, but American fans were still left out of the action. That changed thanks in large part to the efforts of one man . . . and a crew of die-hard riders!

Here Comes the AMA

By the late 1950s and early 1960s, motocross had yet to achieve the status in the United States that the sport had earned in Europe. That's not to say that motocross wasn't popular in America. A small group of American riders routinely competed in AMA-sanctioned races in Grafton, Vermont, and at Sycamore Park near Irvine, California. The first ever AMA race in Grafton was over a 50-foot (15-m) wide and 1.5-mile (2.4-km) long track that surrounded a pasture. Every spectator had a great view.

Americans in Europe

During this period, Americans such as Paul Hunt began visiting Europe to participate in races that were more acrobatic than anything the Americans had seen in the United States. That type of racing caught the eye of Edison Dye, an **engineer** who loved fast cars and faster motorcycles. After watching races in Europe, Dye had an idea that would change the face of motocross in America. In the early 1960s, Dye brought American racers to Great Britain. It was during those visits to Europe that Dye

(above) Belgium's Roger DeCoster was the top rider in the world in the 1960s. Here, he shows off his skill at taking corners at high speed.

(left) Edison Dye not only brought over fast Europeans, but he also introduced the Husqvarna dirt bike to many American racers.

fell in love with the high-powered, acrobatic style of European motocross racers. It was time, Dye thought, to introduce the rest of America to this very exciting brand of riding.

Torsten Hallman Arrives

Enter Torsten Hallman, a four-time World Motocross Champion. Dye brought Hallman and his Husqvarna to the United States in the fall of 1966. Hallman arrived in the United States and participated in **exhibition** races on the west coast. Race fans loved the exhibitions. They had never seen anyone ride like Hallman. After witnessing the Swede ride, America was hooked. The press couldn't stop talking about Hallman. He became a **media** hero. After one particular race near Simi Valley, California, the newspapers gushed. "The newspapers wrote quite a lot about me and my Husky [bike] after my success," Hallman later told a racing historian. "No one had ever dreamed that it was possible to ride so fast on a motorcycle in motocross."

The British are Coming!

Dye believed that if one European champion could dazzle American motocross fans as Hallman had, imagine what a group of Europeans could accomplish! At that moment, Edison Dye's Flying Circus was born. European riders, such as Dave Bickers, Roger DeCoster, and Joel Robert **barnstormed** across the United States for $240 a race in Dye's Inter Am. For the first time, Americans saw motocross as only the Europeans could deliver it. Their **wheelies** and **cross-ups** amazed the Yanks.

Torsten Hallman arrived in the U.S. from Sweden and rocked the motocross world. His travels gained the sport many new fans.

Hallmann rode the Swedish-made Husqvarna ('Husky') bike to his greatest successes.

9

The American Parade

Top American riders, such as Gary Bailey, began to emerge, inspired by the early visits and high-flying example of top European riders.

The Yanks Come of Age

By the late 1960s, the American media was paying close attention to the sport. Local papers followed the Europeans as they dashed across the country, crushing the American competition. Then one day the Europeans ran into Gary Bailey. Born in South Gate, California, in 1943, Bailey's grandfather owned a motorcycle shop. At the age of 13, Bailey got a 1955 Triumph Cub motorcycle and began riding in races with his grandfather and older brother Bob.

Fireworks at Saddleback

On July 4, 1969—Independence Day—Bailey set off fireworks by becoming the first American to defeat a field of European riders. It happened during a race called the Firecracker Grand Prix at Saddleback Park in California. Bailey scored his victory aboard a British-built 250cc Greeves. On the last lap, Stig Petterson trailed Bailey by a few seconds. Generally, racers concentrate so much when they are riding that they never hear the roar of the crowd. But as Bailey and Petterson battled for the win, the American could hear the fans shouting "Bay-Lee, Bay-Lee." "I knew that if I didn't win that race I would really let everybody down," Bailey later told motorcycle racing historian Ed Youngblood. Bailey won, and *Cycle News* reported at the time that "Gary Bailey on his 250 Greeves burned like an Independence Day rocket and beat some of the best racers Europe had to offer, showing the improvement America has made in motocross racing."

Gary Bailey soared to the front of the U.S. motocross pack in 1969 when he became the first American to beat the top European riders.

Moto Fact

Today's motocross racers have trainers to help keep them fit. That wasn't always the case. Gary Bailey was one of the fittest American riders in the1960s and 1970s. Bailey didn't work out in a gym. Instead, he earned a living as a grocerystore warehouse manager. Carrying heavy crates kept Bailey in shape.

Other Racing Series

Before the AMA came along, there were several ways that top American riders got a chance to test themselves. The Trans-AMA series began in 1970, and took place at various courses in the U.S. Dave Nicholl from England was the first winner of that eight-race series. The first year, riders took part in four 250cc and four 500cc races over the course of several months. In following years, they raced as many as 12 times on 500cc bikes. After 1978's events, the series got a new name, and soon AMA took over as the organizer of the top series.

As the sport grew, fans began to pack courses like this one, Saddleback Race Park in the desert of southern California.

High Octane: 1970s and 1980s

As the sport reached new fans and found new places to grow in the United States, a boatload of new motorcycles and a long list of new competitions fueled the riders' abilities and the fans' interest. Motocross was ready to make its next big steps in America.

Japanese Bikes Hit the Dirt

By the early 1970s, the Americans started to do things their own way. Track designers broke tradition when it came to design. Engineers and **mechanics** tinkered with the bikes, trying to make the machines faster. Spurring the motocross boom in the United States were the Japanese motorcycle **manufacturers**. Japanese companies, such as Honda, began selling bikes in the United States. The Japanese models were lighter, less expensive, and easier to ride than the bigger machines from Europe and the United States.

World Competition

As motocross picked up speed in the United States, the young drivers still wanted to prove themselves on the world stage. Fielding a team to compete with the world's best in premier events such as the Trophee des Nations and the Motocross des Nations was difficult. The Americans began fashioning teams for international competition in the early 1970s. In 1972, the team of Gary Jones, Brad Lackey, Jim Pomeroy, and Jimmy Weinert failed miserably, finishing in seventh place during the team world championship.

Brad Lackey, on a Kawasaki motorcycle, won the 1972 AMA national championship. He was also on the unsuccessful U.S. team at the Motocross des Nations.

The Americans mounted several other attempts during the 1970s, but for various reasons, the Americans were never much of a threat. Then in 1981, Danny LaPorte, Donnie Hansen, Johnny O'Mara, and Chuck Sun carved out a place in motocross history. They upset the Europeans in the Motocross des Nations in Beilstein, Germany. It was the most exciting day in American motocross history as the Americans came from behind, beating the British. The Americans dominated for the next 13 years.

(above) Motorcycles from Japan like this Kawasaki were a big reason why American riders began to excel in the 1970s and 1980s.

(left) Big crowds packed the Motocross des Nations tracks to watch the world's best compete in a team format. The first American win came in 1981 in Germany.

High School Motocross

Football games. Basketball games. These sports are popular at many high schools. In the 1970s, a group of high school athletes strapped on their helmets, and jumped on their bikes to ride on a high school motocross team. In the 1970s, high schools across California began forming motocross teams. The idea began with just a few schools. At Inglewood High, students asked the school administration to hold a motocross event on school property. Before the students knew what was happening, workers turned the school's athletic field into a motocross course. For a variety of reasons, high school motocross disappeared. But for one brief moment in the 1970s, motocross heroes got the same attention as the school's star quarterback.

Supercross on the Edge

In 1972, the infant sport of supercross took its first steps. Although races were held in stadiums in Europe, one race in California kicked off the sport Motocross has become.

The Super Bowl of Motocross

Holding a motocross event inside a stadium was the idea of racing promoter Michael Goodwin. Goodwin **christened** his 1972 race at the Los Angeles Coliseum the "Super Bowl of Motocross." The first race included some of the hottest riders around, including Europe's best. Today, MX course designers make sure that **supercross** tracks have tight U-turns and series of so-called "whoops." These are closely spaced jumps that act much like the knee-pounding **moguls** in snow skiing.

Supercross

Supercross is the highest level of competitive motocross racing in the world. To become a supercross champion, a racer must participate in a series of heats, or preliminary races. The top finishers in each of those heats square off in the main race. Those that do not qualify during preliminary heats are given two more chances to make it to the final event. While outdoor motocross races use a timing device to determine who wins, the first racer over the finish line in supercross is the winner.

(above) Fans get to meet with their heroes and learn more about the motorcycles they ride during pre-race visits to the pit area.

(left) Motocross and supercross shows are about more than just racing—stadiums like this one in California put on spectacular shows that include fireworks, music, and more.

Supercross Rocks

The races are a fan favorite—part rock concert and part sporting event, complete with music and fireworks. Before the races, fans meet their favorite racers in the pits, where they can take pictures and ask for autographs. While watching supercross, they get to enjoy extremely fast and aggressive racing, almost constant jumping, and even some mind-blowing tricks.

At the start of a supercross race, racers rev their engines and wait for a gate to drop. Once it does, the dirt flies and the racing starts!

All-Time Winners in supercross (250cc)

Pos.	Rider	Home	First Win	Total Wins
1.	Jeremy McGrath	Encinitas, CA	1993	72
2.	Ricky Carmichael	Havana, FL	1997	48
3.	Ricky Johnson	El Cajon, CA	1984	28
4.	Bob Hannah	Carson City, NV	1976	27
5.	Chad Reed	Australia	2002	26

(Through the end of 2007)

15

It's Showtime !

If there was one person who put supercross on the front page of America's newspapers, it was Jeremy McGrath, whose amazing accomplishments set a pretty high standard for future riders.

Jumpin Jeremy

In the 1990s, MX superstar Jeremy McGrath earned his nickname "Showtime" for performing some of the most mind-blowing tricks ever performed on a motorcycle. His trademark move—the 'Nac-Nac'—thrilled thousands. McGrath's famous maneuver involved moving one leg off of the bike's **footpeg** and swinging it to the same side as the other leg, all the while soaring above the track on his bike. It was a trick that astonished fans and riders.

From BMX to Motocross

McGrath transformed the sport and rewrote the record books. He learned his trade on **BMX bikes**, creating a show like no other rider. Many believe his patented Nac-Nac helped spawn **freestyle** motocross. During the 1990s, McGrath was the chief spokesperson for supercross, appearing on such television shows at NBC's *Tonight Show with Jay Leno*.

Attendance Soars

When McGrath raced, the fans came out to watch. Attendance soared during his years on the supercross circuit. Television ratings for supercross also spiked, and more and more corporations began **sponsoring** individual supercross racers. One of McGrath's most memorable races came during the main event of the Camel supercross series in Anaheim in 1993. At the time, McGrath was a 21-year-old Honda rookie who stunned the field by beating his teammate, supercross champ Jeff Stanton. More than 55,800 motocross fans watched McGrath win his first major victory. "I was pretty nervous at the beginning," he said after beating Stanton. "But once I got that big lead, things went pretty smoothly."

Jeremy McGrath gets some big air and demonstrates a "whip" move.

Jeremy McGrath

Hometown: Encinitas; California

Nicknames: Showtime; MC

Major Achievements:

Motorcycle Hall of Fame
Inductee, 2003

AMA Pro Athlete of the Year, 1996

AMA 250cc National Motocross
Champion, 1995

AMA 250cc supercross Champion,
1993, 1994, 1995, 1996,
1998, 1999, 2000

AMA 125cc West supercross
Champion, 1991, 1992

Motocross des Nations winning
team rider, 1993, 1996

X Games Gold Medal: Moto X
Step Up, 2004

Few athletes have had as much success in their sports as Jeremy "Showtime" McGrath.

No matter where he rode or what he rode, McGrath almost always found himself above the competition.

Ricky Carmichael: The Most Wins Ever

If fans thought they'd seen the best while watching McGrath, they were forced to think again when Ricky Carmichael came along. Carmichael set new records in MX, earning one of sports' greatest nicknames in the process.

The Next Superstar

Ricky Carmichael, who retired in 2007, had the most combined wins of any rider in the history of motocross and supercross. His stellar career was highlighted by two perfect seasons in the AMA Motocross Championship series—he won every race they ran! Carmichael began racing when he was five. His first bike was a Yamaha 50 Tri-Zinger, a gift from his parents on Valentine's Day. At school, Carmichael felt a bit awkward, but on the bike, he was a different person, confident and powerful. He rode in his first race at the age of five. By the time Carmichael was 16, almost everyone who followed the sport knew he was unlike any rider they had ever seen.

Championships All Over

Carmichael collected 67 championships as an **amateur**. He turned **pro** in 1996 when he was barely 17 years old, finishing the year in eighth place and taking home Rookie of the Year honors in the 125cc class. The championships kept coming throughout his career. He won 10 national championships in motocross as well as five supercross series titles. He was also the AMA athlete of the year three times and helped the U.S. team win the important Motocross des Nations international event in 2000, 2005, and 2007. Though he stood only 5'6" (1.6 m), Carmichael stood all alone atop the leaderboard

That's right, Ricky…you're number one! Though he has left his riding career behind him, no one can take away his two perfect seasons and other amazing achievements.

at his retirement. He became the all-time leader in wins with 150 victories. His nickname of G.O.A.T.—Greatest of All Time—was well earned.

On to NASCAR

Carmichael retired from motocross in 2007 to race stock cars. If Carmichael wondered who would succeed him as the next superstar of the sport, all he had to do was take a quick look behind him. The next big name in MX was racing up the charts to try to take on the heroes who had come before him.

Carmichael was able to succeed at any speed. The former MX and supercross champ hopes to add car racing to his long list of championship finishes.

Ricky Carmichael

Hometown: Clearwater, Florida

Nicknames: RC, G.O.A.T. (Greatest of All Time)

Major Achievements:

AMA Pro Sports Athlete of the Year, 1996

AMA Pro Racing Motocross Rookie of the Year, 1996

AMA Pro Athlete of the Year, 2001, 2002, 2004

AMA 125cc National Motocross Champion, 1997, 1998, 1999

AMA 250cc National Motocross Champion, 2000, 2001, 2002, 2003, 2004, 2005, 2006

AMA 250cc supercross Champion, 2001, 2002, 2003, 2005, 2006

AMA 125cc East supercross Champion, 1998

Motocross des Nations winning team rider, 2000, 2005, and 2007.

James Stewart: Loving It !

James Stewart started going fast when he was very young, and he has never stopped. Though still very young, he's already among the best ever.

Bubba Bubbles Up

James "Bubba" Stewart was closing in fast on Carmichael. It was September 2006, and Carmichael and Stewart were battling at the Glen Helen Raceway in Devore, California. On lap six, with Stewart chasing him, Carmichael skidded and spilled his bike. The accident occurred on one of the most **treacherous** courses in motocross. The hills at the raceway were among the steepest in the sport. That accident allowed Stewart, then a 20-year-old from Florida, to pass Carmichael and ultimately win the race, his third victory in the 12-race motocross season. As Stewart accepted the trophy, Carmichael was nursing a bruised shoulder. "I had a good day," Stewart told reporters afterward. "I'm bummin'. It's a lot different out there without my buddy Ricky."

Daring Rider

Stewart, known as "Bubba" to his friends, is one of the most daring riders in supercross. He is also a pioneer of sorts—the first African American to win a major motocross championship. Blazing speed and daring are Stewart's hallmarks. He has motocross in his blood. In fact, his father took him on his first motorcycle ride when he was only two days old. Stewart's father and his mother, Sonya, determined early on that James Jr. would become a motocross champion. "James has a God-given talent and we wanted to give him the opportunity to take advantage of it," Sonya Stewart said in an interview with *Minneapolis Star-Tribune.*

(above) The young motocross rider they call "Bubba" soared over the competition to capture his first AMA supercross title in 2007.

(left) Along with his many indoor successes in supercross, Stewart also is an accomplished outdoor motocross rider.

Young Racer

Stewart entered his first race when he was four years-old and had his first **sponsor** at age seven. The Stewart family went from race-to-race traveling in a motor home. He and his brother, Malcolm, didn't attend regular school. Instead, their parents taught them at home. As an amateur, Stewart won 11 national titles plus dozens of other important events. Anyone who saw Stewart at the time knew this young man was the next big thing. He had all the skills to achieve greatness. In 2002, Stewart turned pro, winning Rookie of the Year. While Stewart is one of the fastest motocross riders on the track, the young and high-spirited successor to Ricky Carmichael was no stranger to injury. "Sometimes, I find myself just smiling like an idiot when I'm racing," he told a reporter. "I don't even know I'm doing it. But I can't help myself. I love it."

James Stewart

Hometown: Haines City, Florida

Nickname: Bubba

Major Achievements:

AMA Sports Motocross Horizon Award, 2001

AMA Motocross Rookie of the Year, 2002

AMA 125cc National Motocross Champion, 2002, 2004

AMA 125cc West supercross Champion, 2003

AMA 125cc East supercross Champion, 2004

AMA supercross Champion, 2007

Here, Stewart shows how riders must lean their bikes during turns, often putting their foot down to help them stay balanced.

The Rider Rules

Football players will sometimes damage a knee. Basketball players might break a wrist or two. But lose a kidney? Break a back? In the sport known as freestyle, such injuries are common, and in many cases, a badge of honor.

Life in the air

Just ask Brian Deegan and Mike Metzger, the two riders who practically invented the sport in the 1990s. Deegan lost four pints of blood and a kidney in 2005 after trying to perform an unsuccessful backflip. Metzger has sustained a series of concussions (where the brain strikes the inside of the skull), a broken back, and other injuries. In the mid-1990s, Deegan and Metzger appeared in videos, jumping and doing tricks off natural terrain. The videos were popular, and before Deegan and Metzger knew it, they were participating in freestyle exhibitions. Soon a touring show motored, or more accurately, flew into local stadiums. The first motocross freestyle competitions were held in 1996. Three years later, at the 1999 X Games, a made-for-TV contest, freestyle motocross made its debut.

(above) Riders use pits filled with foam blocks to help them practice tricks. The foam cushions their landing and lets them walk away to try again!

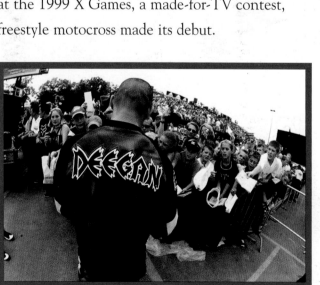

(left) Freestyle rider Brian Deegan is probably telling these young fans, "Hey, kids, don't try these tricks in your backyard!"

Points for Style and Daring

Unlike traditional motorcycle racing where there's a **checkered flag** at the end of each **heat**, freestyle motocross judges award points for style (how good a rider looks while performing), the degree of difficulty for each trick, how well the tricks flow from one to another, and originality, or how different each performance is from the others. The origin of many of the freestyle tricks can be traced back to BMX freestyle riders. For example, there's the Cliffhanger, where the rider leaves the bike in midair, hooks his feet under the handlebars, and raises his hands above his head.

Don't Do this at Home: A Few Freestyle Tricks

360: The rider launches the front wheel of the bike off the ramp, twisting the bike so that it spins all the way around before landing.

Backflip: Launching skyward, the rider pulls the front wheel back until he flips the bike entirely over before landing.

Nate Adams demonstrates one of freestyle's most daring and dangerous tricks, a midair flip. He makes it even trickier by taking his hands off the handlebars!

23

Travis Pastrana: The Freestyle Kid

What goes up must come down. It's the law of gravity. There's no shaking it. But Travis Pastrana tries to defy gravity every chance he gets. Whether it's the X Games, the Gravity Games, or other freestyle motocross events, Pastrana is the king of the backflip, and the most well-known freestyle rider ever!

Travis Pastrana gets muddier competing in racing instead of freestyle competitions.

Upside Down Rider

Not only is Travis Pastrana a super-successful freestyle MX rider, he was also briefly a top rider in motocross, winning both amateur and professional championships. Still, Pastrana's passion is soaring 30 feet (10 m) in the air, sometimes upside down with nothing but a motorcycle between him and the hard Earth. When he's upside down, the motorcycle is between him and the sky, and there's nothing between him and the ground. Born in Maryland, Pastrana got a minibike for Christmas when he was only four years-old. It didn't take long for the young Pastrana to learn to ride. His dad then built a small motocross track on the family property.

X Games to the Max

When Pastrana was 15 years old, he walked into the 1999 X Games in San Francisco and turned freestyle motocross on its ear. Pastrana had ridden well during the event. At the end of a run, Pastrana rode around a jump, set his sights on another jump and hit the gas—launching his bike off a pier and into San Francisco Bay.

When he surfaced from the Bay, Pastrana pumped his fist high into the air. The crowd was forever hooked and wildly applauded Pastrana. ESPN executives weren't amused, though. They gave Pastrana the gold medal, ESPN fined the young rider $10,000—the amount he would have taken home for winning the event.

Broken Bones and Rally Cars

When Pastrana competed in freestyle, he seldom went an entire season without crashing. By the time he was 17, he had already broken more than 25 bones and had undergone eight operations. He is now involved in rally car racing, and unlike other freestyle riders, Pastrana does not sport tattoos, listen to heavy metal music, or curse. He worked extra hard in high school so he could graduate two years early and enroll in college. "I scare myself every day I get on a motorcycle," he once told an online reporter. "I think you'd have to be a complete idiot not to be frightened when you think you're going to crash."

Bold, daring, inventive—that's what has made Travis Pastrana an international superstar in freestyle riding. Finding him upside down like this is not unusual!

Travis Pastrana

Hometown: Annapolis, Maryland

Major Achievements:

AMA Sports Motocross Horizon Award, 1999

AMA Pro Racing Motocross Rookie of the Year, 2000

AMA 125cc National Motocross Champion, 2000

AMA 125cc East supercross Champion, 2001

Motocross de Nations winning team rider, 2000

X Games Gold Medals: 1999, 2000, 2001, 2003, 2005 (2), 2006 (3)

MX Girls

Though up until recent years it hasn't seemed that way, MX isn't a sport just for the boys. From MX's early days to today's top events, women have found a place on motorcycle seats. Today, however, not only can they ride . . . they can be champions!

Pioneer Women

Women have been riding fast and hard since the 1940s, when they tore up the ground on such British bikes as Velocette and Matchless 500s. Yet, it wasn't until the late 1960s that the women's movement in motor sports shifted into high gear in the United States. A handful of pioneers, such as Lynn Wilson and Mary McGee, began participating in desert racing.

Kerry Kleid Trail Blazer

The women, however, had to contend with more problems than the men ever dreamed of dealing with. When Kerry Kleid was 21, the Rye Brook, New York, native became the first woman to be issued a professional motocross license by the AMA—but it wasn't without a fight. While most female riders wouldn't think twice about the license today, it was a big deal in 1971. At the time, Kleid applied for a regulation AMA license so she could enter an all-male competition in upstate New York. The AMA took her license away though when they learned Kleid was female. The AMA thought that 'Kerry' was the name of a male racer.

The stunning Sue Fish, just a teenager at the time, won the first Powder Puff National. She is considered a pioneer of women's motocross.

That is why they granted Kleid a license. Kleid couldn't compete that day, so she took the AMA to court. Kleid dropped the **lawsuit** when the AMA gave back her card. It was a major victory for all female motorcycle racers. In 1974, 9,000 fans watched 300 women racers compete in the Powder Puff National Championship. A year later the event's name was changed to the Women's Motocross Nationals. In 1981, the top 10 women riders appeared at the Los Angeles Coliseum supercross, where 70,000 fans gave them a standing ovation. Female motocross was here to stay.

26

Loretta Lynn Goes Moto

Chiara Fontanesi was all smiles after winning the 2007 AMA Amateur National Motocross Championship at Loretta Lynn's Ranch in Tennessee. This young motocross racer from Parma, Italy, posted three first-place motos in the Girls 9-13 Class. Winning at Loretta Lynn's is no easy feat. The event is the premier amateur motocross competition in the world. Moreover, the Girls' and Womens' classes are becoming more popular with racers.

It's a long way from Italy to Tennessee, so it's a good thing that Chiara Fontanesi didn't have to ride her motorcycle the whole route. She just waited until the last bit, where her skills earned her a 2007 title.

The first Powder Puff National race in 1974 saw hundreds of women race in front of thousands of people for the first time ever.

The Machines

Motocross riders are only as good as their bikes. The machines they ride have changed from rough-and-tumble ramblers to high-tech monsters.

Early Rides

Motocross bikes were not always the sleek speedsters you see on the track today. A German engineer named Gottlieb Daimler built the first gas-powered motorcycle in 1885. That motorcycle resembled a gigantic bicycle more than a sleek road-hugging machine. When British scrambles became popular in the 1920s and 1930s, the bikes weighed as much as 400 pounds (181 kg). These mechanical dinosaurs had virtually no shock-absorbing **suspension system** to smooth out the bumps and dips of the early racecourses. Not only were these machines weighty, but riders found them very difficult to handle. Often times, racers would have to get off their bikes in the middle of the race to push their machines through mud holes. In 1930, the Husqvarna Company of Sweden built a bike that racers could use only for scrambles.

Here's a Honda CRF-450R four-stroke motorcycle being put through its paces by Andrew Short.

The Specialracer Motocykel was heavy and hard to maneuver, yet it was the first attempt by a motorcycle company to cater to the needs of the scramble racers.

Two-stroke Engines

Just before World War II began in 1939, companies in France, Italy, and Germany began developing scramble bikes of their own. These new racing bikes were stronger and more dependable.

28

They could better withstand dirt, rocks, and bumps than earlier models. The seats were wider and more comfortable. Riders could now shift gears using their feet instead of taking one hand off their handlebars. Once World War II was over in 1945, engineers began designing sleeker, faster, motocross motorcycles. The biggest technological advantage during the post-war period was the invention of the **two-stroke engine**. Previously, **four-stroke engines** powered motocross machines. The two-stroke engines made the bikes easier to handle and faster.

Supermoto Action!

Supermoto is a cross between motocross and road racing. Supermoto bikes are generally **single-cylinder**, four-stroke with wheels that top out at 17 inches (43 cm). The rear tires are often hand grooved to allow for better acceleration on the dirt portions of the supermoto course. Supermoto bikes can handle a crash well. Riders are often able to re-enter the race after taking a spill. That's what happened to Jeremy McGrath during the 2005 X Games. At the time, Chad Reed grabbed the **holeshot** and led for the first two laps, with Doug Henry not far behind. As Henry looked for a way around Reed, McGrath motored

Supermoto riders have to conquer not only the rugged dirt tracks, but smooth asphalt roadways like this one.

through the field. He found himself on the floor on the second lap, however. McGrath would not be denied. He spent the next 32 laps chasing Henry and Reed. McGrath and his Honda came in second. Had he had a few more laps to go—McGrath might have won first place.

Moto Fact

While Gottlieb Daimler is credited with building the first gas-powered motorcycle in 1885, American Sylvester Roper invented the first (but short-lived) steam engine motorcycles in 1867.

Japanese Motorcycles

As the 1960s dawned, two-strokes were in and four-strokes were out, although a few drivers still plied their trade on the four-strokes. Japanese companies, such as Suzuki and Yamaha, entered the motocross market with vast numbers of lightweight, two-stroke bikes. When the Americans took over the sport in the 1970s, the challenge for racers and motorcycle builders was to come up with the lightest and most compact two-stroke engines possible. These bikes needed to be more powerful and faster. Slowly, the Japanese manufacturers overshadowed the dominance of the European motorcycle companies.

Environmental Issues

In the 1990s, governments such as California began passing regulations that effectively banned two-stroke engines from the road and open-course competitions, such as desert races. The **exhaust**, or smoke, generated by these engines fouls the air and adds to **pollution**. The two-strokes burn fuel **inefficiently**, causing **environmental** problems. Although the closed-course events, such as motocross, were spared from these regulations, bike manufacturers began to focus on a new generation of cleaner-burning, four-stroke machines. Today, every rider uses four-strokes in the 250cc and 450cc classes.

The Japanese motorcycles, like this Suzuki from 1975, were the bikes of choice for riders like Billy Grossi.

Other MX Gear

Motocross gear has come a long way since the days of the British scrambles. Much of today's riding gear is made from space-age materials designed to keep the rider safe and provide for maximum high-speed performance. Today's racers now wear helmets, gloves, deflectors and protectors made from many high-tech substances. Some helmets, for example, are fashioned from **fiberglass** and carbon. Fiberglass is heat- and fire-resistant. Glass fibers are woven tightly together. Creating the gear is also a science.

Engineers design the shells of the helmets to absorb impacts. The energy generated by an impact is **diffused**, or spread out, before it reaches the driver's head. In addition, some helmets and motocross chest protectors are made of Kevlar, a super-strong material woven together like a tight spider web. Some bulletproof vests are made of **Kevlar**. Body suits are made from comfortable and breathable mesh with additional protection areas for the chest, shoulders, elbows, and upper arms. Some suits feature a hard, removable, plastic breastplate designed to keep the rider safe.

Today's riders benefit from high-tech materials for their protective gear. Helmets like these protect riders'' heads, necks, and faces.

31

Glossary

amateur A person who is not paid to do a job or take part in a sport

BMX bikes Small, gearless bicycles ridden over bumpy dirt tracks

checkered flag Black-and-white checked flag waved at the end of a motor sports race

cc Abbreviation for cubic capacity, which relates to the size of a motorcycle engine

engineers Experts who design mechanical things

exhibition A performance of a sport that doesn't count toward regular standings or point totals

footpegs Footrests on the bottom portion of the bike frame

freestyle A motocross competition in which drivers are rewarded for performing a variety of jumps and aerial tricks

holeshot The space at the first turn of a race that gives a rider the best advantage and the lead in the race

lawsuit Legal process in which two people or companies meet in court to settle an argument

manufacturers Companies that build or make things

mechanics Experts who make engines run properly

media People who work for newspapers, magazines, Websites, and radio and TV stations

moguls In skiing, rugged bumps that skiers go over

promote Organizing and paying for the production of an event

sponsor A company that pays an athlete or team to wear its logos and promote its products

supercross The highest competitive level of indoor motocross racing in the United States

treacherous Very dangerous

Index

32

Printed in the U.S.A.